Legacy Letters

LEGACY
Letters

Discovering the Three
Principles to Personal Health,
Wealth and Wisdom

A SHORT STORY OF TRANSFORMATION

TONY DILEONARDI

NEW YORK

LONDON • NASHVILLE • MELBOURNE • VANCOUVER

Legacy Letters

Discovering the Three Principles to Personal Health, Wealth and Wisdom

Published in New York, New York, by Morgan James Publishing. Morgan James is a trademark of Morgan James, LLC. www. MorganJamesPublishing.com

The Morgan James Speakers Group can bring authors to your live event. For more information or to book an event visit The Morgan James Speakers Group at www.TheMorganJamesSpeakersGroup.com.

ISBN 9781683506270 paperback
ISBN 9781683506287 eBook
Library of Congress Control Number: 2017909500

Cover Design by:
Rachel Lopez
www.r2cdesign.com

Interior Design by:
Chris Treccani
www.3dogcreative.net

In an effort to support local communities, raise awareness and funds, Morgan James Publishing donates a percentage of all book sales for the life of each book to Habitat for Humanity Peninsula and Greater Williamsburg.

Get involved today! Visit www.MorganJamesBuilds.com

A GIFT

of a small book for big change…

To: _____

From: _____

To my brothers,
Michael R. and Martin J.

TABLE OF CONTENTS

CHAPTER 1

Jim's Crisis

February 8, 2008

The headline below the fold in the February 8, 2008, edition of *The Wall Street Journal* read, "Two Convicted in $70 Million Retirement Investment Scheme." The article detailed how Scott B. Hollenbeck and Laurinda Holohan were convicted in a sophisticated fraud scheme targeting elderly investors. The folded newspaper sat on the corner of the desk, still unread by its distracted owner.

Jim Peters sat at his computer, angry and concerned, as he reread an email from his supervisor at a large financial brokerage firm. The smell of pizza wafted into his office, telling him it was midday and yet another financial product salesperson was conducting a meeting in the conference room near Jim's office. No doubt, she was touting her firm's new mutual fund and explaining why the brokers in Jim's office should invest client money. She would likely inform the money managers that her firm's fund had outperformed the S&P 500 stock index the last three quarters. Jim was glad he was too busy and distracted to listen to her and scarf down the free pizza.

He squinted at the screen, not because his eyes were failing him, but because he was frustrated, confused, and wondering what to make of this latest demand from corporate leadership regarding the business, his future, and the care of his customers.

Jim had been a stockbroker at his brokerage firm for thirteen years, following a short stint after college working in a small community bank. He knew the banking and brokerage business very well and excelled at it as he built his business. Jim's firm was one of the largest on Wall Street; for years, he prided himself on his association with the firm and his ability to create wealth for the clients he served. This year, 2008, had started off as strong as previous years for Jim, and he continued to hold his top production ranking in the downtown Philadelphia branch.

Previously, he felt strongly that one of his competitive advantages was the firm itself, providing him the tools, training, and insight to be successful. Those opportunities were the reason he sought employment there many years ago. The admiration had faded recently, however, as Jim grew frustrated with his firm. This email requiring new and different levels of production added to his dissatisfaction.

Jim considered his concerns and wondered to himself if he needed a change. Had he lost confidence in his firm and their aggressive approach to grow business and attract new clients? Or had he lost confidence in himself, in his ability to serve clients in a new, competitive culture? He wondered if his unique way of doing business still worked. Did performing with a high level of integrity still matter? He wasn't sure what his customers expected of him now.

Jim grew up loving competition, math, and numbers—big data it was called today. He later discovered he was made for the financial institutions business, and he loved the fast-paced, highly competitive business and the active, exhilarating markets of which he was a student. Recently, however, he was feeling more like a slave to them.

This email followed several phone conversations with his regional supervisor and a handful of meetings with his branch manager—all of which gave Jim an overwhelming sense of angst. He felt pressured, and for the first time in his career he feared he was about to go down a path of no return. He was not sure he could continue to fight off demands from his superiors and hold at bay the younger, more aggressive advisers sitting in the "bull pen," ready to pounce on his business and his status in the firm. He was conflicted.

The email before him detailed the continuous push he and his colleagues were under to cross-sell more of the firm's own financial products. Jim despised selling only his firm's products, even though those products paid him a higher commission. He prided himself on being a free and independent thinker, and he wanted his customers to trust him to do what was best for them, not himself.

He was repulsed at being pushed to cross-sell products he had no commitment to—

especially when not in his client's best interest. The pressure was mounting, and this latest correspondence brought the issue to a more personal level.

The email stressed the current initiative of cross-selling as a straightforward strategy: "You have a customer who enjoys product A. Why not also sell him your product B? That makes complete sense, assuming suitability is in order," the manager stated in his email—as if the reader was unaware of what cross-selling meant.

Cross-selling products is particularly lucrative in retail banking and brokerage because the most expensive part of the customer relationship is getting a client as a new customer. So the idea of selling as many products as you can to your existing customers is particularly lucrative to the firm and to the individual sales professional. "And, again, there's nothing wrong with this in principle. It makes sense for the company and for the sales professional; the customer can always choose not to buy," the email concluded.

The investment business culture had changed, and in February 2008 Jim felt the high-pressure sales culture that had settled on his firm. Other employees, friends in his own Philadelphia office, were given impossible sales quotas to reach; they were berated or even fired for not meeting them. And so the pressure to cut corners grew, and Jim felt himself wavering.

Jim saw many branch managers routinely monitoring employees' progress toward meeting sales goals, sometimes hourly, and sales numbers at the branch level were reported to higher-ranking managers as many as seven times a day. Tension about how to meet the sales targets was common.

Two hours before Jim received this latest email, he was in a heated conversation with his own branch manager. "Jim, I'm telling you, your past performance does not guarantee any future success," the manager exclaimed. Jim was incredulous. "You need to sell more of our products to your current customers. You need to open fifteen new accounts per quarter, Jim. C'mon, man, we have shareholders to answer to," the manager concluded as he left Jim's office.

At that moment, Jim actually thought about leaving—and not just for the day. For the first time in his career, he thought of leaving the firm. "But what would I do without a job right now?" he muttered to himself.

He recalled his own advice to other young, struggling brokers in the past. "It's better to look for a job when you have a job" had always been his mantra. *I can't leave now. We have real expenses, a big mortgage, and tuitions staring me in the face*, Jim thought. He leaned back in his chair, put his hands behind his head, and looked away from the email. Out his window was the intersection of Market and 17th Streets;

a light, wet snow was falling, and downtown workers scurried through the gray, cold streets. *Where would I go next?* he thought.

Jim was at a crossroads: he could do nothing, ignore the demands from above, and risk his job and possible humiliation, or he could simply give in. "Find a few smaller clients who won't care that you've sold them more of our own cooking," he remembered the veteran broker across the hall saying.

Later that day, just prior to the four o'clock market close, Jim read another email, this one promoting a firm-wide competition rewarding advisers who hit a certain level of production in the current quarter with an all-expense-paid trip to Florida, full of golf and fishing. Jim hit the delete button with disgust.

Weary with worry, he decided to go against his own best judgment, cave to the pressure, and open up a new, albeit fraudulent, account.

"They want new accounts?" Jim muttered aloud, pounding away at his keyboard. "What difference does it make if my dear old aunt opens an account today?" he mused. "She trusts me and will support me, and I will keep her information safe from these vultures."

Jim rationalized that since his aunt was a real person—and very much alive—and since he had no intentions of trading securities in the account, it was all right to open it without her permission.

The first fraudulent account was the hardest for Jim to swallow. The next few that quarter became easier for him to rationalize. After clicking his cursor to submit, Jim shut down his computer, slammed his calendar book shut, and went looking for leftover pizza.

Discussion Questions:

1. *How have you been tempted at work to go against your better judgment? What was the situation?*

2. *What were the outcomes of those decisions?*

3. *What could you have done differently?*

CHAPTER 2

Change and Hope

September 21, 2012

The first signs of fall 2012 engulfed Walnutport, Pennsylvania, on the twenty-first day of September as a cold rain lightly fell to earth. It was a chilly, damp start to the day. Marilyn Peters, who had just spent another hurried morning getting her children off to school and seeing to her elderly live-in mother, grabbed her mug of tea. The smell of spiced apple hit her nose as she began the long journey up the steep, narrow, uneven stairway to the third-floor attic of her newly purchased stone house, almost two hundred years old. She still was not sure if she loved this house in the Lehigh Valley, seventy-three miles northwest of Philadelphia and fifty-six miles north of historic Valley Forge.

Marilyn's steps that morning were filled with the burdens of the last few years. As the middle-aged mother of three and wife to Jim, she was overwhelmed as she tracked up the steps to recover, for the first time, the old wooden box left in the attic by whoever occupied the house before. With each slow step, Marilyn's anxiety grew. Tears welled up in her eyes as she thought about her children, wondering if they were safe at school in this new community, here just a month. As she climbed the steps, she couldn't help but think about why and how the family had ended up here.

Marilyn thought of her husband, Jim, a financial adviser who in 2008 invested his clients' money—among other questionable investments—in levered auction market preferred securities. These "riskless investments" went the wrong way, and several of Jim's affluent clients lost millions of dollars, as did Jim and Marilyn themselves.

Jim's desire to rebuild his business from near bankruptcy led him to leave his large Wall Street brokerage firm of seventeen years and join a small holistic wealth planning boutique firm in Bethlehem, Pennsylvania, just a few miles from Walnutport. There, Jim felt he could go back to helping his customers manage their money without the pressure that came with a large public investment company.

Marilyn ached with guilt as she thought of her quiet doubt and recent lack of confidence in her husband. Were the dark, periodic thoughts an occasional flash of frustration with Jim, or was it more serious? How could she think her love had waned? What started more than twenty years ago as a roaring flame of excitement and passion had experienced a challenging test since

Jim's difficult business decisions. She secretly and desperately hoped this move would reignite his career and also rekindle their love, now a dimming flicker.

Jim's career was definitely a factor in moving to this particular place, at this particular time. Jim wanted to rebuild his practice, and his own personal wealth was of keen interest. Marilyn was anxious for her children to be in a safe environment, and this consideration was perhaps the number one reason they had left Berwyn, Pennsylvania, their affluent neighborhood, and their highly taxed school district.

Marilyn had been troubled by the drug use occurring in Berwyn among the students. Furthermore, she and Jim, both well educated, had grown frustrated with the curriculum changes and dangerous trend of "political correctness" overtaking the public school system.

It worried her when traditional, historical teachings were abandoned and discarded as either untrue or irrelevant. It frustrated her that hundreds of innocent words and phrases—which had stood the test of time—if used by students now, would lead to expulsion. Words like *mankind, religion, poverty, God, slavery,* and even *hunting*. Additionally, birth control was made available to senior high students under the banner of enlightenment. *How did it come to this?* she wondered.

Jim and Marilyn feared for their children's safety and education, and they also feared not being able to afford their education going forward, given their current financial situation.

As Marilyn approached the top of the attic steps, exhausted from months of struggling to stay happily married, raise children, and fund education and retirement costs, her exhausted mind drifted to her mother, Ellen, now slipping deep into Alzheimer's. Bringing Ellen into the spacious old house with the rest of the family was also part of the decision to move, but how much longer could Marilyn care for her aging mom? How much more would this awful disease, which ravaged her mother's mind and purpose, take?

It seemed to Marilyn that only days ago she had lost her father to a sudden heart attack. However, the fact hit her again: it was nearly three years ago that her father, on the eve of his seventieth birthday, unexpectedly passed away. Her mother's Alzheimer's diagnosis came within months.

Marilyn also thought of Jim's sister Karen, living in Akron, Ohio, who was recently diagnosed with stage two breast cancer. Marilyn worried for Karen's health and the care of her two beautiful young daughters. She loved Jim's sister as if she were her own sibling.

She felt sick to her stomach for a moment as she considered all that had occurred recently.

She felt the urge to scream but didn't have the energy. Marilyn wept as she walked into the attic and saw the old wooden box, about the size of a bread basket, sitting on the attic floor—right where it had been since they moved in.

She realized the antique box had been left in the attic soon after closing on the new property. They had bought the old house in a rushed short sale, hoping this less expensive house—a "fixer upper," removed from their old life—would somehow change their fortunes.

Marilyn had walked past the old box, made of cypress wood with a diamond-shaped inlay on the top and two small brass hinges screwed to its side, many times as she stored Christmas decorations and family mementos in the attic. Numerous times before today, she thought about looking into the box but had neither the courage nor the curiosity. The past few weeks had been a desperate, rushed, and stressful time in her life.

Today, however, as she thought about the move, she secretly hoped the unknown contents of the box would somehow create family wealth for generations. Perhaps it was an abandoned treasure, with priceless jewelry left behind. She hoped the box contained old stock certificates and bonds worth millions of dollars. She dreamed of an instant and permanent solution to their financial problems. She had seen pictures of antique stock certificates and bonds at her husband's office; she had also seen shows on TV in which priceless heirlooms were discovered among piles of old junk.

Marilyn was overcome with the smell of must from the old attic; the dust tickled her nose. As she bent over, physically and emotionally exhausted at half past eight in the morning, she was embarrassed at her fanciful thoughts. It was silly to seek wealth in an old box. "How stupid this is," she said aloud as she considered abandoning this scheme.

But finally, like a moth to a flame, she could not help herself or hold back her excitement that perhaps in this old abandoned box she would find something to change her life forever. Little did she know, she would.

Discussion Questions:

1. *How have you felt overwhelmed by your current situations?*

2. *In retrospect, were the overwhelmed feelings justified?*

3. *In what ways are you feeling out of control now? How are you addressing those feelings?*

CHAPTER 3
The Letters
September 21, 2012

As Marilyn drew the antique box from the floor of the attic, she saw her mother's old wooden rocking chair stored in the corner, right where it was placed after moving Ellen into their new house. Her mind flooded with memories of sitting in that rocking chair on her mother's lap, listening intently to classic stories her mother read, like *Curious George* by H.A. Rey and *Make Way for Ducklings* by Robert McCloskey. Oh, how she missed her, the real her; Alzheimer's had turned Ellen into a shell of who she once was.

Marilyn placed her half-empty mug on the floor. The smell of spiced apple wafted out of the mug as she leaned back into the rocker. She placed the antique box on her lap and slowly opened it. Dust fell from the lid, although one could hardly tell where it hit the dirty floor.

As Marilyn looked into the box, she immediately spotted papers—old, yellowed, and curled on the edges. She carefully moved the papers to see if anything lay beneath. Discovering there were just three old sheets of paper, all with artistic handwriting from a fountain pen, she separated the letters and surveyed the top of each. What she saw took her breath away. The top letter was dated October 28, 1789. She curled it back to see the second letter, dated January 31, 1790. And finally, she eyed the third, March 20, 1790.

Marilyn replaced the three antique sheets back into the box and tucked it under her arm. Forgetting her mug, and with heart pounding, she bolted down the stairs like a child at Christmas and dove into her seat at the kitchen table.

Now, seated comfortably and with sufficient light, Marilyn examined the letters more closely and began to read them.

28 October 1789

Dear Sir,

It was such a joy to me to receive your letter. I know we have disagreed on many ideas, yet as I deliberate my own life's work and passions, a most useful adventure for all, I count it an unsuccessful quest that you and I have not yet reconciled. I know our differences are vast, but our passions are similar. It is in that spirit that I wish to share with you now.

Good sir, your letter indicated your high level of disagreement with my well-publicized belief in what makes mankind successful. As I near the end of a most rewarding life, I would like to be sure you are clear on my beliefs.

Success, my good fellow, is fleeting. I would like to tell you the keys to acquiring health and well-being for the individual, who will, therefore, help create success for an entire nation.

As I learned in years of service and thought—and in particular while privileged to serve in France, with the high-thinking French society, where we secured a needed military alliance at a critical time—certain virtues, yes, virtues, once mastered, will account for a life of success and well-being.

Those virtues include temperance, that is, to eat not to dullness, nor drink not to elevation.

And in the discipline of order, if all your acquisitions have their right place and each of your endeavors has the appropriate time, you will find peace. Sunday, as example, is my study day, given over to peaceful, thoughtful, enlightened activities.

Moderation, man, will serve you well. My endeavors of passion—such as love of music, particularly, and love of the game of chess—add greatly to my healthy spirit when practiced in a meaningful moderate way.

The virtue of justice will indeed create health and well-being. Wrong none by doing injury or omitting the benefits that are your duty. My convictions on good health are not limited to me, the individual, but extend to all people groups. This is why I abolished my slaves, for all men should be free to live a life of well-being.

And, finally, the virtue of tranquility— that is, to not be disturbed by trifles or by accidents common or unavoidable—will additionally set one up for a healthy life. Therefore, as I have long stated, a life of daily prayer is a healthy life. We must not forget that powerful Friend, or do we imagine we no longer need his assistance?

In summary, sir, the artistic endeavor of mastering a grateful heart while being thankful will cause long life. The most difficult treasure of mind is that willingness to achieve forgiveness. When achieved, it is well with the soul.

No man can live alone, separated from his favorable community. As you recall, when I was considerably younger, I created and organized a group of like-minded aspiring artisans and tradesmen who hoped to improve themselves while they improved their own community. That organization still exists today and has grown. In that spirit, I wish you peace, good health and well-being. Fondly and respectfully,

B.

Marilyn's mind wandered. Who wrote this? Who was it written to? Why? She felt like she was intruding on a personal drama from many years ago. Excited, she continued with the second handwritten letter.

31 January 1790
Dear William,

I read your last letter with great interest, and even pride, in our points of agreement. For it is true, we have several points of disagreement, made very public by both our works. Again, in the spirit of enlightenment and my desire to make certain you are aware of my true beliefs of what creates success, in this letter, I would like to address the quest for wealth, which many undertake.

Indeed, if undertaken honestly, it is a noble adventure worth seeking. It also is one poorly labeled by many, for wealth lies not only in earthly goods and possessions, but in friendships and experiences. Furthermore, true wealth is uncommon.

Again, the obtaining and maintaining of virtues will set a man on a course of wealth creation. While starting a newspaper, I discovered and implemented the virtue of frugality, that is making no expense but to do good to others or yourself while wasting nothing. Readership in those publications grew at a tremendous rate.

The virtue of industry, dear William, will set a man up for success, while he loses no time, being always employed in something useful. I started the first library due to my desire that the great pastime of reading books might be shared, if we were to pool funds to obtain books for all to share, which we indeed achieved.

Resolution—that is, resolving to perform what you ought, while performing, without fail, what you resolve to do—will never fail you. As example, the invention and discoveries made by mankind come not because of chance or luck, but rather, because science and discovery come from resolute beings who try and try.

Wealth, dear sir, is also derived from the virtue of moderation, the ability to avoid extremes. One must know when and what is enough. And order—the virtue of letting all your achievements have their own place, each part of one's business receiving its due time—is an indispensable part of the wise man's life. As I have said, I'd rather go to bed without dinner than to rise in debt. One must keep one's house in order.

Finally, again, the virtue of justice will never let one down and, strangely, can contribute to one's wealth creation. In great commerce, wrong none by doing injury or omitting the benefits that are your duty. As I have publicly noted, as we enjoy great advantages from the inventions of others, we should be glad of an opportunity to serve others by any invention of ours; and this we should do freely and generously.

Yes, practiced virtues, my son, will lead a man to a wealthy life. You have read for yourself, true godliness with contentment is itself great wealth.

In summary, the art of building true wealth demands one build discipline in all of one's behaviors, which become habits. The truly wealthy human will grasp and learn the fleeting art of contentment. The battle remains an internal one. Ultimately, there is no greater force for the human spirit to achieve wealth than that of purpose. One must discover one's purpose to truly be wealthy. By failing to prepare, you are preparing to fail.

Poverty often deprives a man of all spirit and virtue, dear William. 'Tis hard for an empty bag to stand upright. Peace and wealth to you, my son.

Most fondly and sincerely yours,

B.

Marilyn grabbed her iPad from the kitchen counter. Putting together a few words she gleaned from the letter, she typed "William France 1790" in her search engine. Safari hummed and shot back an article about the year 1790 in France. This didn't seem helpful. She scrolled down and found a timeline of French history, still no help.

Then she added "French 1790 inventors" to the search box on Safari, hoping this would add to the search. Articles on Dr. Joseph-Ignace Guillotin and websites about Louis Pasteur popped up. Marilyn scrolled down, becoming frustrated.

She added the phrase "started the first library" in place of "French 1790 inventors." As her eyes scrolled down to the updated search result, an audible yelp came from her throat and she involuntarily covered her mouth with her hands. She was surprised and excited by what she saw and tapped the link with her finger. It read: "The Library Company: Benjamin Franklin, a printer by trade, a scientist by fame, and a man of action by all accounts, continues to shape American thinking."[1]

Marilyn grabbed the last letter and read it.

20 March 1790
My beloved Son,

    Today I am certain your view of success and the human condition needs one more perspective. What defines the successful life? I have shared with you my beliefs in obtaining good health for an individual, as well as a nation; for creating long-lasting, true generational wealth; and finally, now, pursuing personal wisdom through education, a topic I personally cherish. Tell me and I forget, teach me and I remember, involve me and I learn. William, an investment in knowledge always pays the best interest.

Wisdom, as you know and undoubtedly have heard me say, is the offspring of a virtuous life. An educated life is a life of pleasure; it is obtained by careful consideration and mastering the following virtues.

Silence. Yes, William, silence is a virtue, that is, to speak not but what may benefit others or yourself. This is truly a difficult pursuit for any man. I am reminded of the difficulty firsthand. It is no wonder Holy Scripture warns repeatedly of the tongue.

In my work as an inventor, publisher, and newspaperman, I experienced the virtue of silence as the golden rule on several occasions. I also experienced when

I was unable to practice such, to a failed conclusion.

Another virtue of the enlightened, educated man is sincerity. Sincerity is obtained when one uses no hurtful deceit and thinks innocently and justly. Sincerity, like silence, is difficult to achieve and will be known more in its absence than in its presence. This virtue, like the cracked clay pots of history, will be seen by a viewing world when one is held up to the light where all insincerities and cracks will be illuminated.

An educated person must practice the virtue of humility. A humble student will imitate Jesus and Socrates. Yet, once again, humility, like its sister sincerity, is a very difficult virtue to perfect.

In the quest for education and wisdom, one must also continue to practice the virtues of temperance, order, justice, moderation, and tranquility. An educated person brings forth all virtues to a successful life.

It has been my life's joy to be bequeathed so many wonderful educational opportunities, such as my work with the College of William and Mary, and so many wonderful colleagues, such as Dr. Samuel Johnson and the immigrant Scottish schoolteacher Dr. William Smith.

Recall, son, my dear colleague and patriot Mr. Adam's claim that our prescribed rule of order will only work for a moral and religious people. It is wholly inadequate to the government of any other. I agree, and these virtues will guide you to a self-governed and educated existence. Recall, only a virtuous people are capable of freedom.

Therefore, in summary, dear William, and as we seek reconciliation and understanding, the key to a life filled with wisdom is to constantly seek a new perspective, from many sources, ultimately seeking the truth.

One must also train one's thinking, with discipline and humility. The exercise of the mind is critical for health, wealth, and vitality. Finally, an educated soul will practice the craft of filling one's mind with only beneficial content and information. This will lead to wisdom. Remember, we are all born ignorant, but one must work hard to remain stupid.

As St. Paul stated, ask not whether something is permissible; ask, rather, if it is beneficial.

I have lived, sir, a long time, and the longer I live, the more convincing proofs I see of this truth: that God governs in the affairs of men. If a sparrow cannot fall to the ground without his notice, is it probable that an empire can rise without his aid? We've been assured in the sacred writings that unless the Lord builds the house, they labor in vain who build it. I firmly believe this, and I also believe, without his concurring aid, we shall succeed in this political building no better than the builders of Babel.

May the peace from knowledge and love always guide you on your journey. Hide

not your talents. They for use were made.
What's a sundial in the shade?
Most lovingly, your father,
B. Franklin

Marilyn gasped. She could not sit still. She went to her desktop computer and typed "Ben Franklin's son William." A picture of a white-wigged colonialist popped up with the following description:

> William Franklin (c. 1730–November 1813) was an American soldier, attorney, and colonial administrator, the acknowledged illegitimate son of Benjamin Franklin. He was the last colonial Governor of New Jersey (1763–1776). Franklin was a steadfast Loyalist throughout the American Revolutionary War.[2]

Marilyn read on about William Franklin, both excited and feeling a bit foolish for her lack of knowledge of American history. While she was researching this lesser known Franklin, she discovered the following:

> William Franklin was born in 1730, in Philadelphia, Pennsylvania, then a colony in British America. He was the illegitimate son of Benjamin Franklin, a leading figure in the city. His mother's identity is unknown.
>
> Benjamin Franklin and Deborah Read, his common-law wife, raised William; William always called her his mother. There is some speculation that Deborah Read was William's mother, and that because of his parents' common-law relationship, the circumstances of his birth were obscured so as not to be politically harmful to him or to their marital arrangement.
>
> William Franklin completed his law education in England and was admitted to the bar. William and Benjamin Franklin became partners and confidantes, working together to pursue land grants in what was then called the Northwest (now Midwest).

In 1763, William Franklin was appointed as the Royal Governor of New Jersey, due to his father's influence with the British Prime Minister.

Owing to his father's role as a Founding Father and William's loyalty to Britain, the relationship between father and son became strained past the breaking point. When Benjamin finally decided to take up the patriot cause, he tried to convince William to join him, but the son stayed loyal to the Crown.

William Franklin continued as governor until January of 1776, when colonial militiamen placed him under house arrest, which lasted until the middle of June. After the Declaration of Independence on 4 July, Franklin was formally taken into custody by order of the Provincial Congress of New Jersey, an entity which he refused to recognize, regarding it as an "illegal assembly."

William Franklin surreptitiously engaged Americans in supporting the Loyalist cause.

Discovered, he was held in Litchfield, Connecticut, for eight months. When finally released in a prisoner exchange in 1778, he moved to New York City, which was still occupied by the British. Active in the Loyalist community of New York, Franklin became President of the Board of Associated Loyalists.

In 1782, William Franklin departed for Britain, never to return. In London, he became a leading spokesman for the Loyalist community. Benjamin Franklin became known for his uncompromising position related to not providing compensation or amnesty for the Loyalists who left the colonies, during the negotiations in Paris for a peace treaty. His son's reputation as a Loyalist may have contributed to his position. In 1783 the Peace of Paris was concluded, bringing the war to an end. Parliament agreed to the independence of the Thirteen Colonies and to generous borders.

William Franklin sent a letter to his father, dated 22 July 1784, in an attempt at reconciliation. His father never accepted his position, but responded in a letter dated 16 August 1784, in which he states, "[We] will endeavor, as you propose mutually to forget what has happened relating to it, as well we can." William saw his father one last time in 1785, when Benjamin stopped in Britain on his return journey to the United States after his time in France. The meeting was brief and involved tying up outstanding legal matters.

In his 1788 will, Benjamin Franklin left William virtually none of his wealth, except some territory in Nova Scotia and some property already in William's possession.[2]

Marilyn was stunned, feeling awe in possessing something so significant. She reread the historical letters and then typed "Ben Franklin" into her search engine and saw what she assumed was true. Ben Franklin, one of the Founding Fathers of America, died April 17, 1790. The letters she had in her hand, she presumed, were personally penned to his illegitimate son, seeking reconciliation over conflicting political views, just weeks before he died.

"Wow," she gasped.

Marilyn couldn't breathe. Her thoughts came all at once: *Where did these come from? How did they get here? Who else has seen them? Why did I find them? What can they teach us?* She was no longer exhausted. She was now thoroughly elated—and a bit overwhelmed.

When Jim arrived home later that day from his Bethlehem office, following an urgent, almost frenzied call from Marilyn, he immediately sat with her to look at the letters. Amazed and almost afraid to touch the documents, Jim studied them. He finally looked at Marilyn, who said before he could even speak, "I think they are real; really, I do." Jim wasn't sure.

Later that night, after Jim read the letters again and they discussed who to call and what to do, they considered what Ben Franklin was saying, not only to William, but to them today, with the trials and tribulations they were encountering.

Did these letters matter today—to them? Were these simply letters from a father to his son seeking reconciliation? Or were these letters from a Founding Father trying to explain a larger vision and belief system? After all, Franklin's input heavily influenced the drafting of the Declaration of Independence, one of the most influential documents ever created by humankind. Were these principles his secret to success? Or did they simply convey the sentiments he wished to leave as a legacy to his son?

After struggling through the typical evening duties of preparing dinner, monitoring homework, and cleaning the dishes, Jim and Marilyn talked more and decided not to tell the children about the discovery until they knew what to do next—and whether the letters were legitimate.

Later that night, they retired to their room, where the small flat-screen television was already on. The national news show featured a split screen of five political experts, analyzing and commenting, all talking over one another, about the pending 2012 presidential race. Marilyn urged Jim to "turn off the noise and nonsense."

As Jim reached for the remote control, he heard a ten-second audio segment from a leading political commentator, although Jim was unsure he could name this "expert."

"The key to this 2012 national election," the commentator screamed to be heard over the news show's host, "is which candidate can do more to ease the pains of the American people and provide them with universal health care, more opportunity, better schooling, and greater income." Marilyn again asked Jim to turn off the television.

As Jim acquiesced, a thought came to him. "Marilyn, that's it!"

"That's what?" she retorted.

"The letters! They are the answer to our country's problems. We have been given a precious gift, a reminder from a Founding Father that our solutions do not come from our government, as each candidate is promising this year, but rather the answers must come from the citizens. For years now, we have grown to expect our elected politicians and government to take care of our problems. Well, as I understand what our Founding Fathers envisioned, that's the furthest thing from the truth."

Excited, Marilyn added, "So you think these letters are real? Actually," she went on, without even letting Jim answer, "those letters are not just for William or even for our country now. They are for us as well. You're right; it's our responsibility to care for our family and friends. It's not our elected officials' place; it's not even our government's job. We are 'we the people,' after all."

Jim agreed and added, "As a matter of fact, Mar, our problems are not unique, but to us they are part of *our* daily lives. Who better to solve them than us? Who is affected by our decisions more than we are, and who should care about our outcomes more than us?

"This country was started by people trying to escape tyrannical government, yet, in my lifetime, the size and scope of the federal government has dramatically increased," Jim went on. "Worse, we all assume our elected officials are there to fix our problems; that's how government has gotten so big.

"The federal government decides what kinds of light bulbs I can buy and which doctors I can see. It tells me how fast I can drive and who I must do business with. It's nearly impossible to go to college these days without getting a student loan from the feds, which is ironic, given that federal intervention is what has driven up the cost of higher education in the first place."

Marilyn interjected, "It's no secret many Americans are jaded by Washington. Campaigns essentially are a contest of who can make the best promises to target constituent groups and then turn out the vote among that audience. Supporters of the president embraced expanding the government's role, particularly the executive branch, through executive orders. Of course, they liked who was living in the White House at the time. The other party will do the same when they live there."

"I don't want executive orders, Mar. I want the slow, sometimes messy, process of government and democracy to work as they were intended to. And meanwhile proponents of limited government are called small-minded, unenlightened, and bigots or kooks. I've called people that before and I've been wrong. Perhaps now everyone can understand that allowing one individual to exert unchecked power is wrong, no matter who's in the White House. Our nation was founded on the principle of limited government for good reason," Jim said as he sat back down on the bed.

"The framers of the Constitution, who were willing to die for the cause, did not envision a federal government that imposes one politician's preferences on an entire nation. The federal government was meant to hum quietly in the background and allow us to go about living the lives we choose, without too much intervention," Jim said.

"The founders envisioned a country in which citizens could vote with their feet to live in a state that best matches their values. These flawed but brave men created a document that would have had them hanged for treason, yet it has stood the test of time," Marilyn added.

"And now we have wisdom, in our own hands, from one of those founders. We have virtues to reconsider in our own lives on how we choose to create our worldview and serve each other, regardless of who and what has influence over us," Jim concluded.

"Yes, we need to serve one another," Marilyn said.

The couple thought and discussed through the night. Had they created an environment of sound health, simple wealth, and true wisdom in their home? Did they, along with their children, siblings, parents, and friends, need to understand and reflect on advice from a Founding Father? Was it still relevant advice or just letters for the museum? The magnitude of these thoughts weakened their posture but strengthened their resolve.

Jim and Marilyn thought about their current state: Marilyn's mother, Karen's health, and the kids' education, as well as their own financial future and wellness. Jim cringed as he considered his business and his recent practices. How could they count on themselves, not the government, to live a healthy life? How could they, as a family, create true wealth and manage it? How should they, as parents, educate their children and themselves? How could they create a community that relied on more than government to build a happy and productive life? Whose responsibility was it to deliver happiness? Or was it their right to pursue it? What was "life, liberty, and the pursuit of happiness" anyhow?

They jumped out of bed and ran to the kitchen to read the letters again. This time they read them in a very personal way, to seek guidance for their own current situations. They sought a new perspective on their challenges and hoped insight would come from this Founding Father, a flawed but capable, wise, and visionary man.

They contemplated again the price the Founding Fathers paid for the freedom and independence they were now basking in. They wondered, asking each other, "Is there something here we need to recapture? Should we change our current way of living? Is there a fresh perspective in these historic ideas we can implement today? Do we need to adjust our worldview?"

Throughout the night and into the next morning, Marilyn and Jim talked, cried, hugged, and wrote what they were discovering about each other. They envisioned what was needed to survive and thrive during these difficult times as a family. They considered and discussed their choices to date and the consequences of those choices to their family.

By the next morning, they had created their summary of what the letters meant and what they were saying about living well. Written in

Marilyn's own handwriting, on a yellow legal pad of paper, was the following:

> Healthy, wealthy, and wise! How to achieve it? Discovering the three principles to personal health, wealth, and wisdom.

- **Health**

  The three principles to achieving personal health, defined as being joyful and seeking happiness, are as follows:
  1. Master thankfulness
  2. Choose forgiveness
  3. Create community

- **Wealth**

  The three principles to obtaining genuine generational wealth, defined as freedom to choose, are as follows:
  1. Build discipline
  2. Learn contentment
  3. Discover purpose

- **Wisdom**

    The three principles to achieving wisdom, defined as owning one's choices, are as follows:
    1. Seek perspective
    2. Train thinking
    3. Fill your mind with beneficial content

After Marilyn wrote and edited all the comments and words that flew around the room, she looked at the now dog-eared legal pad with these new principles, and then she looked Jim square in the eyes.

"How do we do this?" they asked in unison.

Discussion Questions:

1. *Who in history would you like to meet and why?*

2. *What would our country be like today if* _____ *(fill in the blank) did not occur?*

3. *Who would you write a letter to today to be read in the future? What would be the main theme of that letter?*

CHAPTER 4

Health and Worry

March 20, 2012

I n March, prior to the hurried, late-summer move from Berwyn and the discovery of the historic letters, when Marilyn first heard from her sister-in-law Karen about her recent diagnosis, life seemed to be spinning out of control for their family. Marilyn's heart sank with the news from Karen about her doctor's visit.

"How far along is it, Karen?" Marilyn asked reluctantly, afraid to even speak the word *cancer*.

As Karen explained the process she had gone through over the last several months, she could no longer hold back. Even though they were on the phone, Marilyn knew Karen was crying. She did not know what to say to her sweet sister-in-law, the girl who had been there for Jim through all these years of life.

Jim adored his little sister and would surely take the news hard. Marilyn thought about how special it was to have siblings, particularly those with whom you share trials and triumphs. Siblings have a unique history with one another, knowing each other in every phase of life. How special it was to Marilyn to be close to Karen and her husband, Ed. But now, with Karen and Ed far away in Akron, Marilyn felt distant, too far away to truly help them in this time of need.

Jim and his sister had grown up in Akron. Jim's parents were committed, active, wonderful, and loving parents. They provided everything their kids needed, including a welcoming, safe home, formal Sunday dinners, and vacations to the Florida Gulf Coast once a year. Jim and his two siblings were active at St. Michael's Catholic Church in Akron, as well as participants in the local park district sports programs.

Jim, who played basketball through high school, was determined to play ball and attend college. He worked hard at grades and athletics. Assuming funds were tight, he believed his parents could only afford one child's college tuition. Jim chose a local community college so Karen, a dedicated student, could go to the state university. Even so, Jim excelled at the junior college, playing basketball and getting his associate's degree in business management. Jim worked hard and soon landed his first job in an Akron-area bank, where he learned the inside workings of financial institutions.

Later, while Karen was away at college, Jim moved to Philadelphia and entered the financial services industry as a fulfillment and mailroom manager, overseeing the daily mailings of fund prospectuses and marketing materials. He continued his education at Temple University at night, eventually earning his bachelor's degree in finance.

Enchanted by the business, Jim was soon promoted to a sales desk position, where he got licensed by the securities regulatory agency and learned the investment business by cold-calling hundreds of prospects a day. He loved talking about stocks and bonds and watching the markets. He took pride in managing clients' money and helping them understand the nuances of investing.

Thinking of Jim and Karen's special bond, Marilyn wept as she hung up the phone, promising Karen she would visit Akron after Easter. How sad she was for Karen, Ed, and their kids. She was truly afraid of what was to come.

Marilyn, a few years older than Karen, made a mental note to see her doctor soon, now with a bit more urgency. It seemed too much time had passed since her last visit, but Marilyn had put off the expense.

She tried to fight back the worry over the cost of a necessary doctor's visit, but every decision regarding money had been stressful since Jim's business suffered during the Great Recession. Years later, there was still much talk as leaders and experts debated how to "fix" the healthcare problems and the rising cost of insurance.

After a few more moments of silent worry, Marilyn finally called Jim at his office in Philadelphia. She told him of Karen's diagnosis. As expected, Jim was speechless. In the background, Marilyn could hear the television blaring in Jim's office, broadcasting the latest chatter about the financial markets and global economy. How she hated the financial news and what it did to Jim's daily mood. The noise and false urgency the headlines created made it difficult to plan long-term or talk calmly about the future. Even in good times, reporters found reasons to claim the sky was falling.

Though the worst of the Great Recession was now history, rebuilding Jim's practice had been a difficult, never-ending process. Recovery tapped all of Jim's optimism and energy, yet he still hadn't regained the money lost more than three years ago.

It seemed to Marilyn everyone would be better off without the financial news, a sentiment Jim did not agree with. Jim said he would call Karen right away and try to get home early to be with Marilyn. "We need to get to Akron right after Easter," he said as he slammed down the phone.

Thoughts of Karen's illness made Marilyn think of other hard times she had experienced with sickness and death. Of course, her most immediate health concerns were for her mother, Ellen, suffering with Alzheimer's, but she also thought back to her father and his unexpected death.

Tom's death was quite a blow to Ellen, and Marilyn missed her father immensely. Unfortunately, all Tom left Ellen was debt. It took Marilyn and Jim several months to organize and work through Ellen's financial situation after Tom passed. Not only was it a sad loss for Marilyn, but it added to Marilyn and Jim's financial stress as well.

Ellen Leonard was a quiet, strong, and private woman, carefully but adoringly living in the shadows of her vibrant, bigger-than-life husband, Tom. Tom Leonard, Marilyn's beloved dad, was a sales representative in the clothing business for more than forty years. He traveled a lot when Marilyn was young. Marilyn loved her dad, despite his challenges and time away from home.

He was fun-loving and always showed great care and concern for Marilyn. Tom and Ellen

Leonard had built a home in Wynnewood, Pennsylvania, to experience life in the suburbs of Philadelphia in the postwar era. It was a typical childhood for Marilyn, filled with activities, 4-H, craft classes, and swimming lessons at the local YWCA, church events on Wednesday, and Sunday school at the Wynnewood Presbyterian Church.

Marilyn couldn't stop her thoughts from venturing back even further, to the time in her childhood when she lost Christopher, the younger brother so dear to her. Christopher was killed while walking home from school by what the family claimed was a drunk driver. Because of the snowstorm and icy conditions, the crash was deemed an accident.

Christopher was nine years old, and Marilyn was heartbroken. The car slid off an icy road that afternoon, careened off a tree, and hit him. He was killed instantly, but the loss of that day stayed with Marilyn and her parents forever.

While Christopher and Tom represented past hurts, the discomfort of bearing Ellen's diagnosis—and now Karen's—was a very real part of the present. Little things caused her mother confusion and concern. Ellen even had difficulty maintaining a conversation on certain days. To think of it all made Marilyn feel scared and discouraged. Health problems and financial concerns seemed to overshadow all that was good in life.

But, of course, there were also happy times to remember. Early in their careers, Marilyn and Jim both lived in Philadelphia. They first met on a hot July Sunday afternoon in the emergency room, when Jim, dressed in a filthy, sweat-drenched baseball uniform, came in holding his left thumb, hanging awkwardly at a forty-five-degree angle.

Marilyn, a committed nurse and always the professional caregiver, laughed out loud when she saw Jim's thumb and the silly look on his face as he entered the ER. After apologizing to him for the outburst, she asked what had occurred. Jim, with visible pride, told her the entire story of how he jammed his thumb while sliding into home plate at a softball game with his buddies and their park district team, the Traders. "But I was safe!" Jim exclaimed.

They started dating soon after and fell in love. They had so much in common: both loved to travel, loved the outdoors, wanted children, and loved helping other people, Marilyn with medicine and Jim with investments.

Two and a half years later, with Karen and Ed by their side, Marilyn and Jim got married. They lived in downtown Philadelphia while both focused on their careers. Three years later, they had their first child, Emily. Emily was smart, strong-willed, and focused. Two years later, they had William. Will was laid-back and funny. Needing more space, they moved to Berwyn, bought a comfortable home, and settled in. Five years later, their baby, Margaret, joined them. Margaret was special. She was full of love and gave smiles away like raindrops in a summer storm.

Shortly after Margaret was born, Marilyn noticed Margaret had poor muscle tone, and her physical features were different; her neck was shorter than Marilyn's other babies', with excess skin at the back of the neck. Marilyn grew more concerned as she noticed Margaret's flattened facial profile and her small head, ears, and mouth. Margaret had Down syndrome. They soon learned what having a special-needs child can do to a family, yet they also experienced unbelievable joy as Margaret changed their lives.

Yes, Marilyn thought, life is full of happiness and sorrow. *How can I prevent the sorrow from taking over?*

Discussion Questions:

1. *What childhood memories are most precious to you today?*

2. *What would you claim as your worldview? What is your faith position? Where and when were they formed?*

3. *Who are the most significant people in your life right now? Why? Do they know?*

CHAPTER 5

Finances and Family

June 11, 2007

I n the early summer of 2007, Jim had his first glance at what truly lay ahead for the nation—an economic tsunami like nothing he had ever seen or studied. Jim chose a career in financial services initially because he loved numbers. He loved watching and studying the markets, and, honestly, he loved making money. He also enjoyed helping his customers think about their futures and plan for retirement. He took pride in his career and his ability to recall numbers and prices of blue chip stocks from fifteen years ago. He had an impressive memory for that type of activity. He often laughed as he fondly recalled childhood memories of dominating in Monopoly with his friends growing up.

Jim had spent years preparing for this career, studying, training, and learning all he needed to know to be successful and add value to his clients, who trusted him. Not only did he have a photographic memory and sharp mind for the markets, he truly loved diagnosing a client's challenges and opportunities like a skilled medical doctor.

As his business grew and the number of his clients increased, he found it more challenging to serve all his clients in the way he liked. He considered ways to serve his clients in a more "institutional" way—that is, invest clients' money in more institutional products that would not require as much time and research. At first he thought he might be shortchanging his clients. Over time, however, with pressure mounting, he rationalized that even with this new "hands-off" approach, he was doing more good than harm.

As 2007 opened, he realized many of his clients were invested in and taking advantage of the booming housing and mortgage business. Furthermore, he was investing in auction rate preferred (ARP) stock. ARPs are securities with interest rates reset through auctions. Oftentimes issued by closed-end funds, ARPs typically have their interest rate reset on a short-term schedule that ranges from fourteen days to seven weeks.

The ease of participating in these seemingly simple and lucrative investment products, coupled with the US housing bubble, made ARPs hard to resist. However, they took a toll on his clients when everything failed: mortgage crisis, credit crisis, bank collapse, government bailout. These phrases frequently appeared in the headlines throughout the fall of 2008, a period in which the major financial markets lost more than 30 percent of their value. This period also ranked among the most horrific in US financial market history. Those who lived through these events would likely never forget the turmoil.

The events of the fall of 2008 were a lesson in what eventually happens when rational thinking gives way to irrationality. While good intentions were likely the catalyst leading to the decision to expand the subprime mortgage market back in 1999, somewhere along the way the United States lost its senses.

During this turmoil, Jim committed fraud by setting up a dozen fake accounts, which were never funded and had no activity. Additionally, he lost tremendous amounts of investment money for himself and his clients by investing in complicated, risky products—all because he was greedy, lazy, and under tremendous pressure to perform or be replaced.

While Jim lived through the most difficult time in the business, he nearly lost everything. His desire to simplify the products he recommended to his customers backfired. The nation's inability to save, as well as his own desire to spend money he did not have, ended up costing millions in the end.

Jim's clients were cut in half, and his own personal 401k investments were sliced by more than 50 percent. Jim had no idea how he would begin to recoup his practice and his own wealth. Additionally, he could barely look himself in the mirror; he certainly couldn't explain any of this to Marilyn.

Marilyn, on the other hand, had been called to a career in nursing. She loved helping others. Her experiences growing up, compassion for others, and scientific mind created a desire to serve others through nursing. After attending Drexel University in Philadelphia and getting her nursing degree, she took her first job in an emergency room at Thomas Jefferson University Hospital in Abington, Pennsylvania. Even though she was assigned crazy overnight hours, she loved her job. It was exciting, and she felt relevant.

She eventually moved up the ranks, worked even harder, and took leadership roles within the hospital's ER ward. The only aspect of life she enjoyed more than nursing was her family. After she and Jim got married and settled into their new life and careers, they thought about children. It was not long after that Emily was born. Marilyn loved juggling life as an emergency room nurse and a mother.

Over time, however, she recognized it was difficult to do both well. Not only did she long to be with her baby more, she was growing frustrated with the administrative bureaucracy the hospital kept adding to day-to-day operations. It seemed like nurses did more and more work as doctors became more burdened and concerned with how the business of medicine was changing. Malpractice insurance was rising.

When the time came, Marilyn took pride in the decision to leave her career. She felt called to sacrifice her professional desires to raise her children the way she and Jim wanted. Marilyn then became a more active participant in her children's lives, focused intently on their health and education. It was these very issues, however, that caused her so much worry as she settled into life in the new home. In fact, concern for her children's safety and well-being was the very reason she found herself in Walnutport at all.

Discussion Questions:

1. *What is your definition of wealth? What do you need to change your life?*

2. *What three jobs or duties do you enjoy the most in your daily life? What three do you dislike the most?*

3. *What skills set you apart from other colleagues or family members?*

CHAPTER 6
Education and Adjustment
January 16, 2011

In January 2011 at Berwyn Community High School, a seventeen-year-old male student was suspended because—rumors from concerned parents said—he had a handgun in his locker. In addition to being frightened by such news, many parents were frustrated the school district leaders and school's principal were quiet about the circumstances, leading many parents to search for information by any means possible. The community went on a witch-hunt for information on how and why this student had a handgun in school. After several heated school board meetings and PTA meetings, the community settled back into a normal rhythm, realizing no new information would be made available.

This, to Marilyn and Jim, was disheartening. While the school system was one of the reasons they had moved to this community, they had grown frustrated over time. Their three children were getting lost in the large suburban public school system. There were safety and morality concerns, of course, but also a troubling trend toward political correctness over traditional values.

Marilyn, who considered herself an advocate for higher education, was growing more and more frustrated with what she saw happening on college campuses in America. She had discouraging, firsthand information about her own alma mater. As she thought about her children's secondary education, she wondered

what their college education would look like—
let alone cost.

The more Marilyn and Jim got involved in
the public school system, the more stress they
felt. She loved most of her children's teachers
and felt concerned for their care, so she was
frustrated by laws putting more pressure on these
committed educators. She knew many cared
about their students and learning, but these
teachers often felt handcuffed by bureaucracy
and the meddling of special interest groups, all
of which made it difficult for them to teach. Jim
and Marilyn feared these new undercurrents in
education would harm their children.

The final straw occurred when several boys
in Emily's junior high school were suspended
and a coach terminated after reports of an
"extremely disturbing" incident on a bus with
a sports team.

The incident happened as the junior
varsity wrestling team was returning from a

tournament. Sources close to the investigation reported that the incident involved a twelve-year-old boy who was allegedly sexually assaulted by several upperclassmen while on the school bus. Again, very little information was made public to the parents of classmates.

Additionally, Jim and Marilyn both grew concerned about the level of drug use taking hold of their affluent community. Reports, particularly alarming among high school students, suggested heroin use was on the rise. Heroin use, they learned—and Marilyn knew from her work in the ER—often started with abuse of a prescription painkiller the teen found in the medicine cabinet at home.

Life was changing for Jim and Marilyn as their children grew older. They were not quite sure how to solve these community problems, but they felt the need for a change, a fresh start. So Marilyn found herself in an old home in a new community. Her kids were in smaller schools, her husband worked at a new job, and her mother was living with them. She had never felt as overwhelmed as she did on this particular rainy September morning.

Prior to their move from Berwyn and the discovery of the letters, they had been experiencing the trials and tribulations that many hardworking, good people experienced.

Discussion Questions:

1. *What is wisdom?*
2. *Who are your mentors? Who are you mentoring?*
3. *What are your best memories from grade school? High school? Why are they so memorable?*

CHAPTER 7

The Learnings

September 22, 2012

Once Marilyn and Jim got the kids off to school and checked on Ellen, they showered, dressed, and sat at the kitchen table to review their new list of foundational principles and discuss the "how do we do this" question from the night before. Jim called the office and told his assistant he would not be in until after lunch. Marilyn couldn't help but think back, just twenty-four hours ago, as she struggled up the attic stairs, unaware of what she was about to discover, feeling overwhelmed, depressed, and flat-out afraid. Now, just a day later, she was excited and alert—though still wary about their future.

"So, Jim, what should we do now?" asked Marilyn.

"With the letters?" Jim asked.

"No, about us!"

"What about us, Mar? We're fine."

"James, we are not fine."

"Oh, boy, it's James now, huh?"

"Jim, I am afraid. I'm afraid for our marriage. I'm afraid for our children, and I'm afraid for our future."

"What are you afraid of?"

"Losing everything!"

"Everything? Losing me?"

"No, I'm not sure what I mean. I'm just so concerned about our future. I am just so afraid. Look at these headlines!" Marilyn shouted as she tossed the three newspapers sitting on the kitchen table toward Jim.

Jim still loved receiving and reading physical newspapers: the touch, the smell, and the way they folded. "Come on, Mar," he said.

"Read the headlines, Jim. Out loud!"

Jim read, at first mumbling, but as he read more, his voice grew stronger:

Neighborhood Watch Shooter on Trial

When neighborhood watch volunteer George Zimmerman shot and killed 17-year-old Trayvon Martin in Sanford, Fla., it sparked outrage after Zimmerman was not immediately arrested. The shooting raised questions on gun control and racism in America and made one article of clothing (the hoodie) into a national symbol. At the time of writing, Zimmerman faces second-degree murder charges and is slated to go on trial next summer.

13 Dead, 50 Hurt in Colorado

Police said a gunman, with a gas mask on and dressed in black, shot and killed dozens and dozens of people. Authorities say the suspect, James Holmes, 24, killed 10 people inside the theater complex and that three others died after they were taken from the scene.

Inside Sikh Temple Attacker

Wade Michael Page killed six people at a Sikh temple in suburban Milwaukee on Aug. 5 in a rampage that left terrified congregants hiding in closets and others texting friends outside for help.

With Strike over, Chicago Schools Face Another Test

Linking teacher evaluations to student achievement can be a hard assignment, as other states' experiences have shown . . .

"Keep going," Marilyn insisted.

"Come on, Marilyn," Jim snarled. "This is useless."

"Please keep reading," she quietly requested.

"What good is this?"

"Are you truly aware of what's happening out there, Jim?"

"I am!" he said as he reluctantly complied with her request to continue reading headlines:

U.S. Ambassador, 3 Staffers Killed in Libya in Outburst over Anti-Muslim Film

U.S. Denies Obama Snub as Netanyahu Escalates Iran Threats

U.N. Envoy to Meet Assad, Rebels in Syria

Dead Gitmo Prisoner Had Been Cleared for Release, Attempted Suicide

U.S. Marks 11th Anniversary of 9/11 Attacks

UBS Whistleblower Rewarded $104 Million by IRS

Having rattled off these headlines quickly, he asked with frustration, "So what, Mar?"

"So everything, Jim! The world is a dangerous place, and what are we doing about it? What are we doing to protect our family and friends? I am just flat-out afraid!"

Jim looked deep into Marilyn's eyes, held her hand, and calmed himself. "It's always been a dangerous place, honey," he said tenderly. "This is not new to humankind." He suggested she let go of the negativity and not be so afraid. He challenged her but proceeded cautiously, knowing she was vulnerable and emotional. He searched for the right words.

"Marilyn, I think those letters came to you exactly at the right time," he said. "I think you have been tremendously frustrated with me and some of the difficult choices, actually bad choices, I've made over the last few years. Furthermore, I think you are mad at your mom for being sick, mad at your dad for his weaknesses, and even mad at your brother Chris for dying so young . . . Marilyn, stop being so mad at everyone! Just let this stuff go."

Marilyn looked away for a moment, gathered herself, and squeezed Jim's hands. "I don't know how," she said.

Jim grabbed the pad of paper from the table and said, "Let's see what Dr. Franklin has to say to us, shall we? Right here, Mar. This is what *you* wrote. The three principles to achieving personal health, defined as being joyful and seeking happiness, are mastering thankfulness, choosing forgiveness, and creating community."

Jim went on to share with Marilyn how she had created an incredible community for their family. He reminded her of how she cared for them, her mother, and even Karen. He reminded her of all they had to be thankful for: three beautiful, smart, and loving children— one, a special-needs child who had delivered more love than either could have imagined. They had loving, imperfect parents who tried hard to provide shelter, security, and love to them, as they were now attempting to do for their children. They had solid educations and enjoyed relaxing family vacations together. They usually had the means to do most of what they needed to do to survive and thrive.

"Marilyn, the only thing on the list you haven't done is choose to forgive those in life who you feel have let you down," Jim said quietly.

Jim got up and put another pot of water on to boil. "Now, as far as wealth is concerned, here's what Ben says—may I call him Ben?" Jim joked. "The three principles to obtaining genuine generational wealth are building discipline, learning contentment, and discovering purpose. Marilyn, you have always been a person of discipline."

Marilyn earnestly replied, "Jim, you have always been a person of purpose, and for that I am grateful."

"Thanks, Mar, and now both of us need to learn more about contentment. I'm sorry I have been so obsessed with 'keeping up with the Joneses' that I have forgotten all we have been given. I was fooled into believing keeping up was my duty and what you wanted. Through my entire professional career, I have been living as if the grass was greener somewhere else—and I was hell-bent to find it, but that's a dangerous and desperate place to be, Marilyn."

Marilyn drew him closer.

"I can't help but think of one of my dad's favorite quotes," Jim said. "He had it framed on his bedroom wall, but I haven't thought about it in years."

"What is the quote?" Marilyn asked.

"It's by G.K. Chesterton: 'There are two ways to get enough. One is to continue to accumulate more and more. The other is to desire less.' I was always intrigued with that quote but never completely understood it."

"Well, Jim," Marilyn said, "you've heard the phrase 'the teacher emerges when the pupil is ready.'" She laughed.

"Indeed," he added. "You know, I'm not worried about the fact that I have a low feeling of myself or my self-worth. I am actually more concerned that I have a bloated feeling of my self-worth," he whispered. "If you really understand human nature, the bloat is more dangerous to us all."

They talked about contentment and what it meant today. They thought about their purpose as loving parents and caring friends.

Broken, Jim confessed, "Marilyn, I got greedy and power hungry. I lost perspective and rationalized my behavior as good for all. I lost my way, my direction, and my purpose. I let outside institutional influences affect my choices—caused me to do what I knew I should not do. I began to read my own headlines and thought I was above the rules and desired approval from others. How much longer can we spend more than we have? How much longer can our country spend more than we make? I owe you an apology. I owe our kids my time. I owe my clients an apology. Marilyn, please forgive me for putting us at risk," he concluded.

"James, you are forgiven and loved."

He smiled. "Big institutions should not influence our life and personal choices like we have allowed them to. Our worldview should do that. Mar, at least an employer pays you for the services you provide, but a government provides services that we pay for. Why would we worry and count on that model as much as we have?" Jim asked. "We need to liberate ourselves from those institutions' hold on us."

They sat silent for a moment until Jim once again spoke. "Marilyn, do you remember the Bible text read at our wedding?"

"What? Why are you asking me that?"

"It was Luke, something or other," Jim said.

"It was Luke 12:22: 'Then Jesus said to his disciples: 'Therefore I tell you, do not worry about your life, what you will eat; or about your body, what you will wear.'[3] I can't believe you almost remember," she joked. "What about it?"

"Mar, it stayed with me. We need to stop being so anxious about everything. I've been anxious at work, greedy to be on top. You've been anxious with the kids' education and with the health of your mom and Karen. We have to stop!"

"Jim, saying 'Stop being anxious' is like telling a child to stop crying when he just got his feelings hurt or lost that special toy," Marilyn rebuffed. "It's impossible."

"Okay, Mar, Jesus also says to replace anxiousness with something else, doesn't he?" Jim shot back. "Marilyn, we have to have hope. We have to *believe* there's a way out, a better plan. We must replace anxiety with something else. We must have faith in ourselves, trusting we can thrive during tough times."

"You've got a point, Jim, you really do," Marilyn replied.

Finally, Marilyn leaned into Jim and stated the three principles to achieving wisdom she had discovered in the letters: "'Seek perspective, train our thinking, and fill our minds with that which is beneficial.' Jim, we can commit to do this. We can hold each other accountable," she said happily.

"What was it you just said about the teacher showing up? Mar, we need to be lifelong learners. We need to read more. We need to read with our kids more. I need to shut off the news and talk radio and replace it with more enlightened readings and perspectives," Jim stated.

They discussed their new perspective and new way to think about thinking. They laughed at some of the things they had turned into habits, like certain questionable television shows which had become weekly, even daily, hobbies and binges. They determined many of these poor choices were made out of boredom and were not beneficial to them. They evaluated where they got their news and how often they tuned in or sought to read it. They took an inventory of people they wanted in their lives, and some they did not. They considered and reconsidered places they frequented. They criticized how much time they all were spending on screens—computers, phones, and tablets alone.

They discussed what they ate, how they ate, and how they managed stress. Jim tried to remember the last time he played softball or basketball with his buddies or the kids. "Marilyn, when was the last time we went camping or hiking?" Jim asked.

They wrote down short-term goals to make sure they would stay on track, and some long-term objectives to keep them energized. They sought truth.

"Jim, these goals all sound reasonable, simple even, but I am not sure this will be easy," Marilyn said, looking dejected. "Is this practical and sustainable?"

"Mar, let me give you an example of what I'm thinking about and how we can do this. It's a simple example, and I'm a bit embarrassed I've lost touch with it."

"What are you thinking of?" she inquired.

"You know how Ed goes up to Michigan each January with his buddies for a guys-only snowmobile trip?"

"What? How's that an example of taking control of our own life? How is Ed's playtime an example of us living the life we are intended to live?"

"Well, I saw it firsthand the one time I went with them," Jim went on, undeterred. "It was absolutely intriguing. Hundreds of miles of snowmobile trails were available for safe and fun snowmobiling. They are maintained and managed by volunteers. Each town and county has volunteer groups to groom and survey the trails for the ultimate experience. I've seen the people who are taking thorough care of the trails; there are groups raising private funds for equipment. Citizens and enthusiasts alike volunteer their time, talent, and treasure to keep old, repurposed railroad trails safe and enjoyable. They do this for the love of the sport, but they also know what this means to these small towns for tourism and business. Cities compete with each other. Small businesses vie for customers in a healthy, competitive way.

"Marilyn, this type of activity and civic involvement happens every day, thousands of times a day, in every part of our country—without government involvement. That's what we need to honor and elevate each day. We need to protect that idea and embrace it for ourselves. Nobody cares about us like our small community does. We have the most to gain—and lose—by how we interact with our communities effectively, efficiently, and lovingly."

"Jim, that is exciting and empowering. But what do you mean by time, talent, and treasure?"

"It means everything important to us. It means exactly what it sounds like: our priorities and the choices we make each day. We all have twenty-four hours, God-given talent, and resources. Let's refocus those truths on our family and community. If everyone did that, so many problems would soon go away. We need to self-govern first. We know wrong from right."

Jim and Marilyn spent the next several hours talking through their most personal feelings, challenges, and issues. They vented to each other about the feelings of respect and love they had—or didn't have—for each other. They shared bitterness and anger over what had gone wrong throughout their marriage and life. They talked about regrets and what they desired to do differently now.

They envisioned where to spend more time, what issues to discuss more often, and what experiences to share as a family. Marilyn verbally forgave her mother for not being stronger when her father was alive. She forgave her father for not being perfect. She even forgave Jim for his "aggressive" pursuit of money, which he confessed, with a tone of embarrassment, had at times been out of control. They wept and hugged.

They debated each other but ultimately agreed it was time to take full ownership, together, of their lives, not counting on government, but rather counting on themselves, their faith, and the community of family and friends they had created over the years.

As Marilyn leaned into Jim's chest, both of them exhausted and emotional, with the new list she had written on the pad of paper in her hand, he whispered, "Marilyn, for us to thrive is for us to take back control of our choices—our family, our well-being, and our own life. I want to help lead us to live a life of wellness. I want us not to worry about money, but rather redefine and create wealth together, and I want us to raise admirable, God-fearing, and productive adults, not just compliant, well-educated kids.

In whatever I do professionally, I need to create a customer experience that proves I love my customer, whoever they may be."

They began their new journey right then, as they held each other, prayed together—out loud and awkwardly—and recommitted, from that day on, to "do life" together, not expecting so-called experts, elected officials, strangers, or circumstances to dictate their life and, more important, their decisions.

In the days that followed, Jim and Marilyn reviewed their findings and debated and discussed their current situation and how they had gotten there. Nothing, they agreed, was sacred, except their unending love for each other and their children. They agreed every current way of thinking could be challenged, and it was. They challenged every dependency they thought they had.

In no time, they made changes—small ones at first, followed by larger changes to their thinking and their choices. They determined which areas to take more ownership of and responsibility for as they cared for each other, their family members, and their community.

Their confidence grew, their communication with each other increased, and their discussions took on a new, more purposeful direction. They felt liberated from their old way of thinking and their old dependencies. They felt inspired and began to see good in people, more than evil. They took the principles to heart. They debated them, shared them with others, and implemented them in their own lives. They realized they could live the lifestyle of their own choosing, free of outside influences and free to accept the consequences of their own decisions.

Discussion Questions:

1. *Where are the greatest needs in your community today?*

2. *Who serves your community well today? How are they doing it? Why?*

3. *What institutions have an unhealthy hold on you now? What action can you take to weaken that hold?*

CHAPTER 8

The Outcomes: Implementing the Principles

August 17, 2016

I t was a blazing hot, humid day in Philadelphia on August 17, 2016. Marilyn, Jim, and the family left the Benjamin Franklin Museum in Franklin Court, just off Chestnut Street in downtown Philadelphia, where they had spent the day looking fondly on all the historic artifacts in the museum. The history of Benjamin Franklin had never been more real and relevant to Jim as it was now. As the family left the museum and walked toward the parking garage, he was overcome with joy as he considered what had occurred in the four years since he and Marilyn discovered the lost legacy letters and implemented the new principles.

Earlier that week, they celebrated the life of Ellen, who at seventy-six years old passed away after her brave and tough fight with the Alzheimer's disease. She had spent the last four years living in their home. They offered her amazing care, along with community doctors, and the memories were life changing for all. Mainly for her daughter, who, despite the hectic pace of her life, decided to embrace the very difficult burden of caring for a loved one.

Thriving and happy, Jim considered his family standing in front of him and recalled all that had occurred. Three years prior, he had sold his financial planning practice to a younger, tech-savvy financial planner.

Empowered by his desire to make a difference in the lives of young people in his community, Jim was instrumental in starting a private religious high school in a downtrodden area of Bethlehem, Pennsylvania.

He now taught economics and business classes to seniors, mainly minorities and immigrants. He ran the school as headmaster and coached the basketball team. He was busier than ever but loved being involved with these high school students, who had been dealt a tough hand in life.

Along with the profit from selling his practice, Jim's network of colleagues and clients enabled him to raise funds for the school. Two very successful financial advisers from New York City, whom Jim had met during his days in the business, provided substantial funding. These donations allowed Jim to breathe life into his vision of opening the high school in Bethlehem, near the closed steel plant.

Steel Academy, or SA, as it was often called in the community, was a college preparatory private school located in an old pole barn on Mechanic Street, near Lehigh College. On the front of the school appeared this inscription: "Yet true godliness with contentment is itself great wealth" (1 Tim. 6:6).[4]

Over three years, SA developed what some would call an unusual vision for the city of Bethlehem. Its vision included an appreciation for the quality of life and opportunity for success city living afforded, but Jim also desired to see this opportunity made more readily available to all citizens of the community.

Jim and his partners chose the area around the steel plant because of its rich, diverse history and its opportunity for change and growth, especially with respect to the youth in the community. Beginning in 2012, Jim, while still a financial planner, but with an eye on transitioning to something different, started afterschool and summer programs in that neighborhood near the abandoned and turned-over steel factory.

These programs included the Steel City Little League basketball clubs, summer camps, mentor programs, and scholarships for deserving youth. It was a beneficial set of programs to the community, but Jim and the other volunteers came to realize that to truly impact the less privileged kids' lives, they needed a more comprehensive plan and tactic. They needed to develop a full-time academy, complete with academic, spiritual, and athletic instruction. These children needed encouragement and guidance from caring mentors.

It was out of this realization that the vision for Steel Academy was born and continued to develop. Jim and the leadership had outlined their vision and plans for a college and life-preparatory high school. They, along with many gifted and committed people, had given their lives completely to this call.

In the summer of 2013, a group of businesspeople, formed by Jim, purchased the shuttered corporate training facility from Bethlehem Steel and began remodeling it for a school. The facility included meeting rooms, a small auditorium, and a kitchen and dining hall.

With the assistance of hundreds of volunteers, future students, and, eventually, private contractors, Jim and the team began a full year of renovation. Highlights included hosting two hundred volunteers, from New York City high schools and churches in Philadelphia and central New Jersey, who spent their spring break living in the old building, creating a gym floor by night and executing the demolition plan and reconstruction by day. Volunteers made it happen.

Twenty-four students graduated in the first senior class, and 100 percent of the class went on to college in the fall. Most kids in that community would not have graduated from high school.

Marilyn took her love of nursing and passion for cooking and started a local business serving healthy cooked meals for the elderly, shut-ins, single moms, and special-needs families. Her one-person business, HomeBase Partners, prospered to add employees to serve meals and offer in-home care for the ill.

As Marilyn's business flourished, she was extremely busy. Even so, she found ways to balance it all with raising her kids, staying involved in the community, and caring for her mother in her home until her death.

Karen and her husband, Ed, were at the funeral services for Ellen. Karen was in remission and, much to Jim and Marilyn's delight, Karen and Ed had moved to live nearby. Ed moved his plumbing business from Akron to Allentown, just sixteen miles away, to be closer to their dear relatives and friends.

Jim's youngest daughter, Margaret, became part of a disability ministry at Allentown Community Fellowship Church (ACF). The program was called Helping Everyone Realize Our Savior (HEROS). Ed and Karen, along with other caring volunteers, helped start it as they saw it modeled in the Akron area and had a passion and calling to serve these special students in their new community. Even their daughters volunteered to help with HEROS.

The goal of the HEROS group was to care for special-needs individuals and their families, inviting the disabled to worship and serve Jesus and the church body with their gifts. ACF believed that HEROS are created by God for a purpose and are an indispensable part of the body of Christ. The church provided access to worship, ministry, and fellowship for the mentally disabled and their families, both at church and during school.

The purpose of HEROS was clear, as Ed loved to explain: "Whether you're a person with disabilities, someone who loves them, or someone who desires to serve them, there is a place for you here. You are welcome here!" ACF had served more than thirty area families with this ministry, including Jim and Marilyn. Margaret was thriving in school and in HEROS and even had a part-time job in a local coffee shop.

Jim and Marilyn's oldest daughter, Emily, volunteered at Steel Academy and went on to Leigh University, pursuing a degree in journalism. Will, who attended Steel Academy, played on the baseball team and decided to learn a trade, focusing on plumbing. Will often spent time with his Uncle Ed, working for him over the summer break.

As Jim considered the last four years and how far they all had come, he saw how focusing on creating a community, where no one was dependent but everyone was included, could create health, wealth, and wisdom for generations to come.

He considered the letters often as he learned and implemented the three principles to achieving personal health, defined as being joyful and seeking happiness: mastering thankfulness, choosing forgiveness, and creating community.

He also thought of what had occurred in their professional lives and personal financial situation that led them to pursue true generational wealth, defined as freedom to choose. He worked with fervor to build discipline, learn contentment, and discover purpose.

A smile often overcame him as he pondered his life, now so different because he implemented the three principles to achieving wisdom, defined as owning one's own choices:

seeking perspective, training one's thinking, and filling one's mind with that which is beneficial.

As the Peters family waited for the parking garage attendant to bring their car, for their return trip to Walnutport, Jim teased the three kids about where they should stop for dinner on the way home.

"Somewhere with air conditioning," Will bellowed with drama as if he were going to faint. Jim wanted a cheeseburger and French fries with gravy at his favorite Philadelphia diner. Will was demanding fried cheese balls and a milk shake at his favorite burger place. Emily was insisting they go to her favorite organic juice bar for wraps and healthy drinks. Will turned his nose up to that suggestion. And Margaret was urging the family to go back to Walnutport for her favorite pizza joint.

While Jim was playfully arguing with the children, Marilyn looked up to the large flat-screen television behind the parking garage cashier's head. Marilyn's eyes and ears caught a split screen of several political pundits, screaming at one another about the caustic 2016 presidential election. "The key to this 2016 national election," the expert shouted to be heard over the CNN host, "is which candidate can do more to ease the pains of the American people, provide them with universal healthcare, more opportunity, better schooling, and higher income."

Marilyn shook her head and smiled. She turned to Jim, who was on one knee talking with Margaret, and said, "Funny, isn't it? That sounds so familiar."

"What, Mar?" Jim asked as he stood up and turned toward Marilyn.

"Oh, nothing, hun," she laughed. "I just feel like I've heard that before. It really is nothing."

She smiled and returned her attention from the noise of the TV back to her happy, healthy, growing family.

Discussion Questions:

1. *Where and how often do you "view" news? What kind of news? How much time do you spend watching TV?*

2. *What can you change about yourself, your family, your team, your company, and your community today?*

3. *What is your legacy?*

Personal Notes:

Personal Notes:

ABOUT THE AUTHOR

As the founder of Third Quarter Institute, Tony DiLeonardi channels nearly thirty years of sales and managerial financial services experience to help lead, inspire, and guide professionals through the challenges of running a dynamic business today.

Third Quarter Institute is dedicated to helping leaders improve their legacy and their organizations' health. It offers strategic best practices, coaching services, and solutions for C-suite individuals, corporations, family offices, and charities.

Tony speaks regularly at meetings across North America and strives to equip each audience he addresses with the skills and creative thinking needed to enhance their overall business and personal life.

In his corporate career, Tony was vice chairman at Guggenheim Investments and, prior to that, vice chairman, senior managing director of distribution, at Claymore Securities Inc., an innovative exchange-traded fund (ETF), closed-end fund (CEF) firm that was acquired by Guggenheim Partners. Tony also served as a national sales manager in Canada, opening an organization for First Trust Canada.

Tony is the author of *Face to Face: Creating Lifelong & Multi-Generational Clients*. He co-authored the book *The $14 Trillion Woman: Your Essential Guide to the Female Client*.

This is his first novel. He earned a bachelor's degree in communications from Illinois State University and lives with his family near Chicago.

ACKNOWLEDGMENTS

It's always difficult to thank all those involved in this process. I wish to thank the following: Terry Whalin, David Hancock, Margo Toulouse, and Nickcole Watkins at Morgan James Publishing; Angie Kiesling and team at The Editorial Attic; David Goetz, Chase Neely, Rev. J. Brian Medaglia, Dr. Chris Castaldo, John Lorentsen, David Hooten, Shane Michelli, Lou Holland, Dr. Jim Juriga, Paul Negris, Scott A. Moore, Kristan Wojnar, Carl Hass, and Michael Rigert. And mostly, thank you Diane, Thea, James, Emma, and Ellie—you light up my world.

HEALTHY, WEALTHY & WISE

Discover the three principles to personal health, wealth, and wisdom.

- **Health**
  The three principles to achieving personal health, defined as being joyful and seeking happiness, are as follows:
  1. Master thankfulness
  2. Choose forgiveness
  3. Create community

- **Wealth**
  The three principles to obtaining genuine generational wealth, defined as freedom to choose, are as follows:

1. Build discipline
2. Learn contentment
3. Discover purpose

- Wisdom

  The three principles to achieving wisdom, defined as owning one's choices, are as follows:

  1. Seek perspective
  2. Train thinking
  3. Fill your mind with beneficial content

ENDNOTES

1. Independence Hall Association, "The Library Company," The Electric Ben Franklin, http://www.ushistory.org/Franklin/Philadelphia/library.htm.

2. *Wikipedia, the Free Encyclopedia*, s.v., "William Franklin," (accessed Oct 2016), https://en.wikipedia.org/wiki/William_Franklin.

3. Holy Bible, New International Version®, NIV® Copyright ©1973, 1978, 1984, 2011 by Biblica Inc.® Used by permission. All rights reserved worldwide.

4. *Holy Bible,* New Living Translation, copyright © 1996, 2004, 2015 by Tyndale House Foundation. Used by permission of Tyndale House Publishers Inc., Carol Stream, Illinois 60188. All rights reserved.

RESOURCES

If you are experiencing difficulties similar to those our characters faced, there are resources available to you. Here are just a few you may find helpful. Check your local communities for support.

If you or a loved one has been diagnosed with Alzheimer's or a related dementia, you are not alone. For the millions of people affected by the disease, the Alzheimer's Association is the trusted resource for reliable information, education, referrals, and support. www.alz.org

Parents and families of children with Down syndrome can connect with other families from around the world to learn more and share information. The NICHD-led DS-Connect® is a safe and secure registry to help families and researchers identify similarities and differences in the physical and developmental symptoms and milestones of people with Down syndrome, which can guide future research. Learn more about DS-Connect®: The Down Syndrome Registry. www.ndss.org

Breast cancer patients can learn more about care at Cancer Centers of America: www. cancercenter.com

If you are looking for information on home health care services, check out Home Helpers Home Care: www.homehelpershomecare.com.

Looking for financial strategies and resources? There are plenty to choose from, but be careful of your choice. Here are a few we recommend: DaveRamsey.com, Crown. org, MasterYourMoney.com, WiseBread.com, TheMilitaryWallet.com, and DoughRoller.net.

If you wish to read more of Franklin's wisdom, consider his essay "The Way to Wealth," written in 1758. You can access a copy here: http://www.swarthmore.edu/SocSci/ bdorsey1/41docs/52-fra.html.

Share your own helpful resources with others at www.legacyletters.xyz

Share your own legacy letters with others at www.legacyletters.xyz

To order books for your group, please contact us at www.legacyletters.xyz

A REAL OUTCOME OF COMMUNITY AND LEGACY

Proceeds from this book will support Chicago Hope Academy. Chicago Hope Academy is a co-educational, non-denominational college and life preparatory school dedicated to nurturing and challenging the whole person—mind, body, and spirit—to the glory of God.

You can learn more about Chicago Hope Academy and support its efforts to transform the urban educational experience, one student at a time, by visiting www.chicagohopeacademy.org

Morgan James
Speakers Group

www.TheMorganJamesSpeakersGroup.com

We connect Morgan James published
authors with live and online events
and audiences who will benefit
from their expertise.

Morgan James makes all of our titles
available through the Library for All
Charity Organization.

www.LibraryForAll.org

Printed in the USA
CPSIA information can be obtained
at www.ICGtesting.com
JSHW082355140824
68134JS00020B/2088